City

Jared Siemens

Go to **www.av2books.com**,
and enter this book's
unique code.

BOOK CODE

X375393

AV² by Weigl brings you media
enhanced books that support
active learning.

AV² provides enriched content that supplements and complements this book. Weigl's AV² books strive to create inspired learning and engage young minds in a total learning experience.

Your AV² Media Enhanced books come alive with...

Audio
Listen to sections of
the book read aloud.

Video
Watch informative
video clips.

Embedded Weblinks
Gain additional information
for research.

Try This!
Complete activities and
hands-on experiments.

Key Words
Study vocabulary, and
complete a matching
word activity.

Quizzes
Test your knowledge.

Slide Show
View images and
captions, and prepare
a presentation.

... and much, much more!

Published by AV² by Weigl
350 5th Avenue, 59th Floor New York, NY 10118
Website: www.av2books.com

Library of Congress Cataloging-in-Publication Data

Siemens, Jared.
 City / Jared Siemens.
    pages cm. -- (Where do you live?)
 Includes bibliographical references and index.
 ISBN 978-1-4896-3597-6 (hard cover : alk. paper) -- ISBN 978-1-4896-3598-3 (soft cover : alk. paper) --
 ISBN 978-1-4896-3599-0 (single user ebk) -- ISBN 978-1-4896-3600-3 (multi-user ebk)
 1. Cities and towns--Juvenile literature. 2. City and town life--Juvenile literature. I. Title.
 HT152.S56 2016
 307.76--dc23
                          2015013373

Printed in the United States of America in Brainerd, Minnesota
1 2 3 4 5 6 7 8 9 0 19 18 17 16 15

072015
072415

Project Coordinator: Jared Siemens
Design: Mandy Christiansen

The publisher acknowledges Getty Images and iStock as the primary image suppliers for this title.

City

CONTENTS

I live in a city.

4

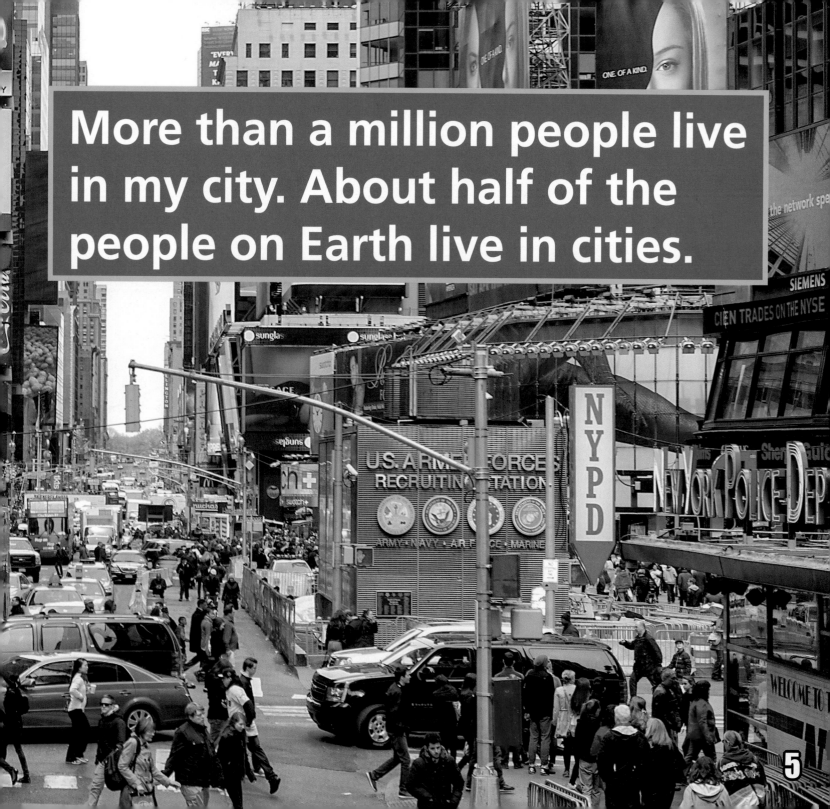

More than a million people live in my city. About half of the people on Earth live in cities.

Cities have very tall buildings.

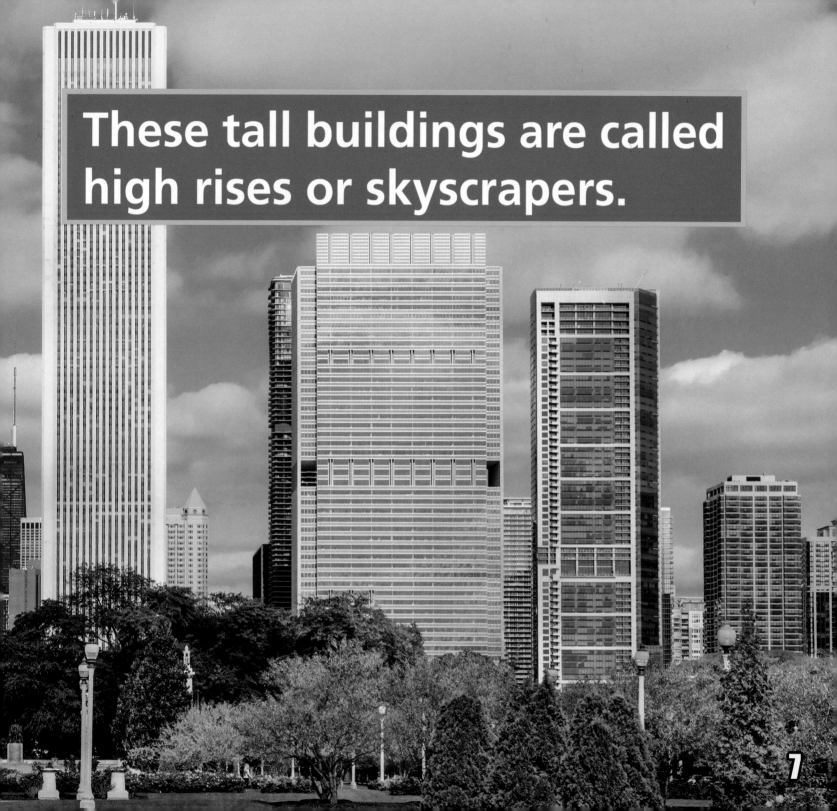

These tall buildings are called high rises or skyscrapers.

My home is in a high rise near the middle of the city.

The cars on the streets below look like toys.

My city has many schools and playgrounds.

The jungle gym
is my favorite part
of the playground.

My city is joined by many roads. Roads help people get to where they want to go.

People in a city can travel by car or bus. Some cities have trains and subways.

13

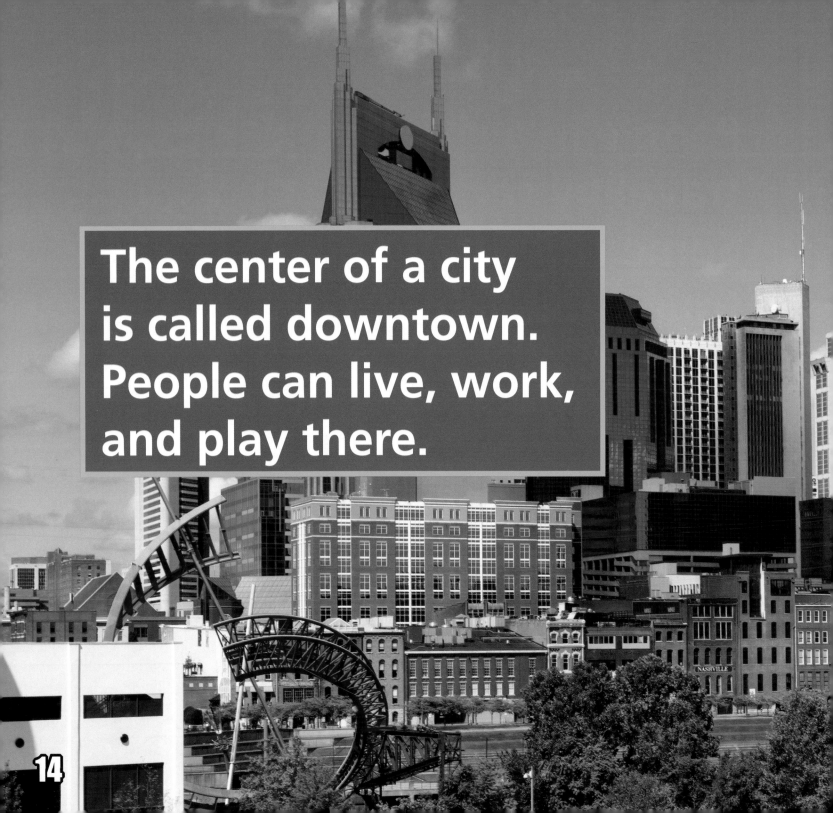

The center of a city is called downtown. People can live, work, and play there.

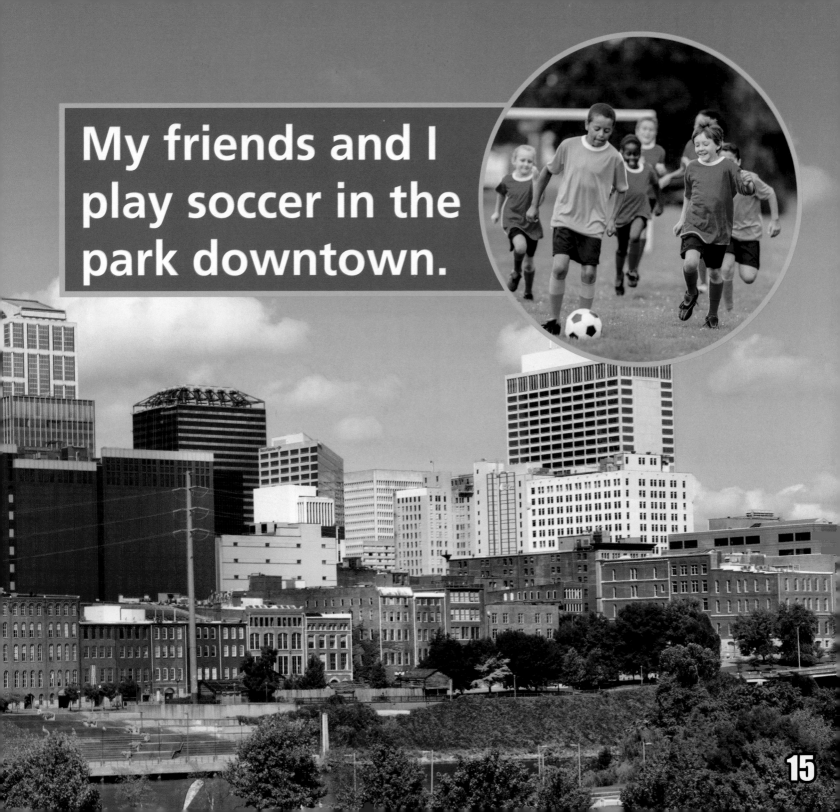

My friends and I play soccer in the park downtown.

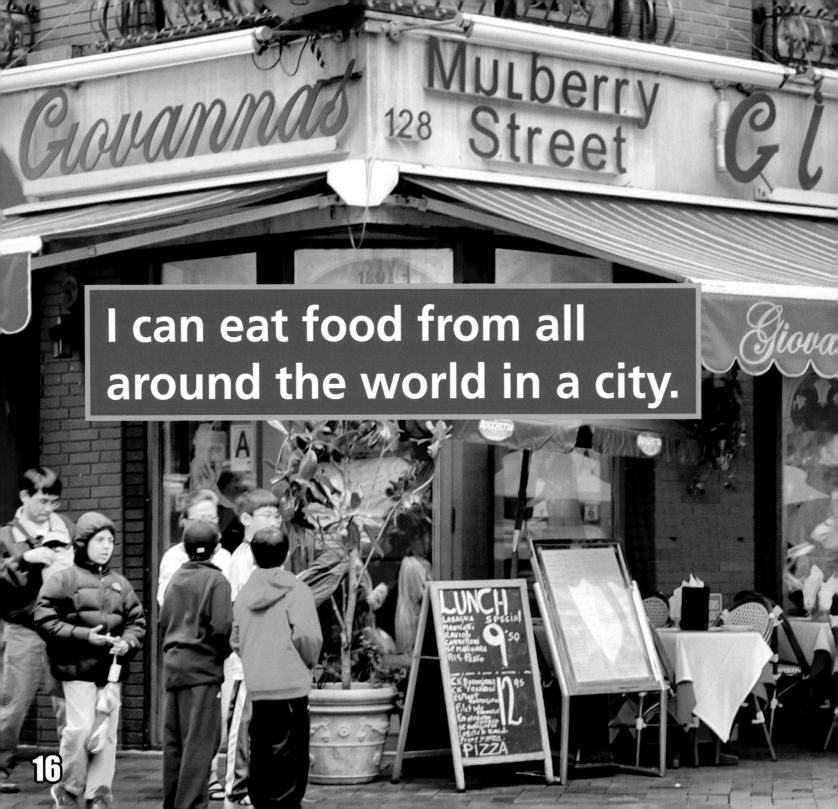

I can eat food from all around the world in a city.

128 Mulberry Street

Giovannas

LUNCH SPECIAL
9.50

PIZZA

16

My favorite foods
are pizza and sushi.

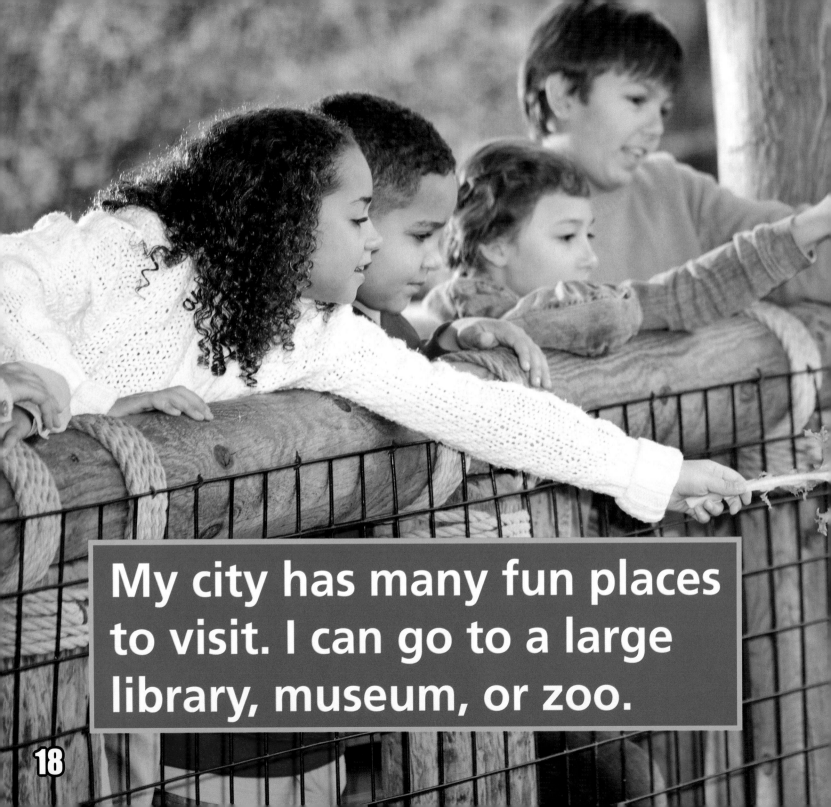

My city has many fun places to visit. I can go to a large library, museum, or zoo.

Monkeys are my favorite animals at the zoo.

19

The people in my city get to vote for our leader.

Ballot

BALLOTS

.ting
oday

VOTE

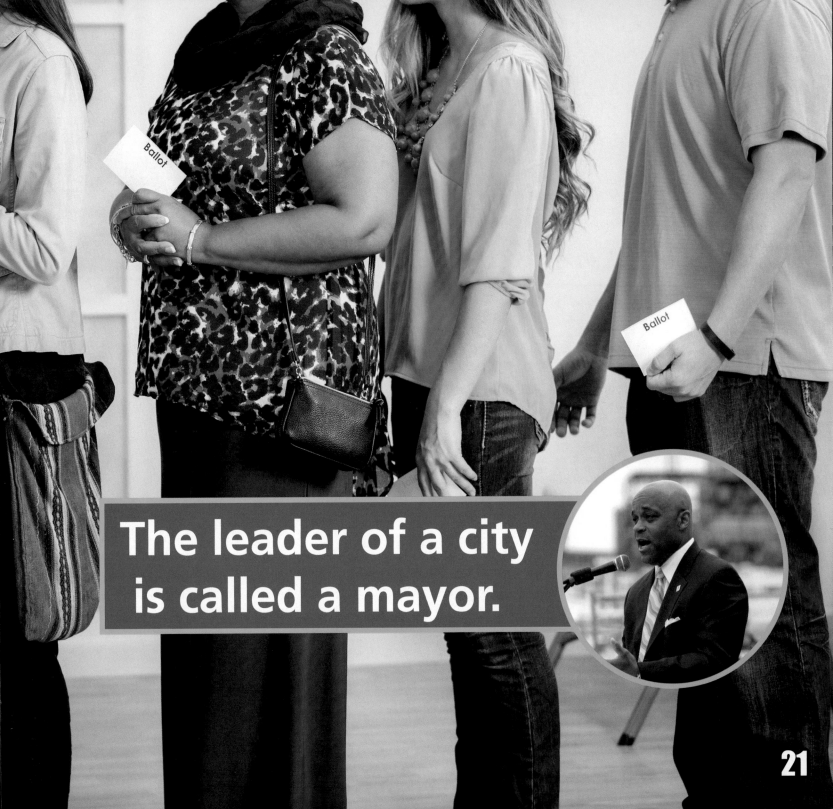

The leader of a city is called a mayor.

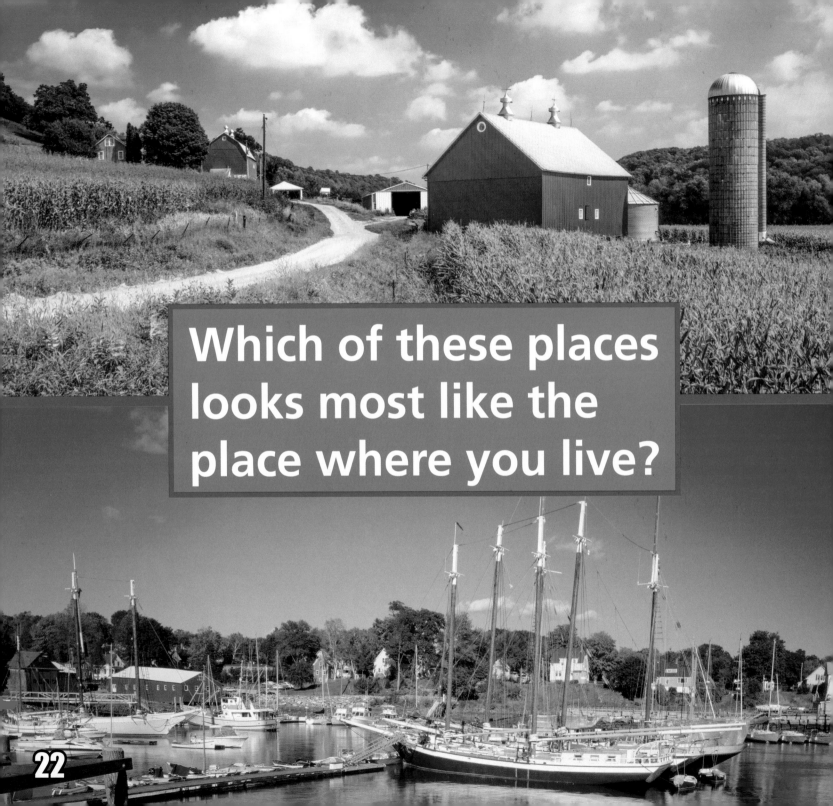

Which of these places looks most like the place where you live?

What is the same?
What is different?

KEY WORDS

Research has shown that as much as 65 percent of all written material published in English is made up of 300 words. These 300 words cannot be taught using pictures or learned by sounding them out. They must be recognized by sight. This book contains 57 common sight words to help young readers improve their reading fluency and comprehension. This book also teaches young readers several important content words, such as proper nouns. These words are paired with pictures to aid in learning and improve understanding.

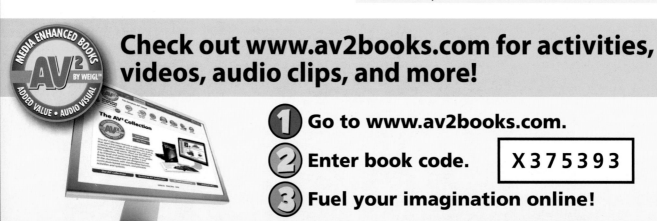